Written by Vicki Spandel
Illustrated by Jeni Kelleher
Layout and Design by Steve Peha

Vicki's photo courtesy of Lynn Woodward, woodwardcreative.com

Thanks to Sneed B. Collard III for his photo of the fritillary that inspired Jeni's painting at the end of Chapter 16.

Printed in the United States of America.

Published by:

Teaching That Makes Sense, Inc.
104 R NC HWY 54, PMB 367
Carrboro, NC 27510

ISBN: 978-0-9972831-3-6

No Ordinary Cat

By

Vicki Spandel

Illustrated by

Jeni Kelleher

Table of Contents

This book is lovingly dedicated to Snooky, who, like the queen she was,

ruled my grandmother's yard in Williston, North Dakota for a remarkable

22 years. During her reign, this legendary hunter took on all comers,

including one very surprised ferret and several arrogant neighbor dogs who

didn't fully appreciate cats until Snooky widened their vision.

Introduction

When my beautiful children Nikki and Michael were small, story time was my favorite part of the day. After the chaos of bath time, we'd settle on our green velvet loveseat, me in the middle holding a favorite book. And Mike, the little one, would often say, "Where were we?"

Now, you don't ask "Where were we?" when you read a picture book. It's over quickly, like a song. But with a chapter book, you don't usually finish. That's the best part really. All those questions, the kind that build in your imagination as you read, linger.

As I thought about this, it hit me—the books I most loved to read aloud to my kids were chapter books. *Winnie the Pooh, The Best Christmas Pageant Ever, The Twits, Charlotte's Web, Abel's Island, Boy, The BFG, The Witches, Matilda, Harris and Me, The Wind in the Willows,*

Emmett Otter's Jug Band Christmas, The Tale of Despereaux, and on and on. All had a special place in my heart. Why?

Maybe because when you read a chapter book, you live inside it for a time. The characters become your friends. Their dreams, wishes, and worries become yours, too. The settings where they reside become your world.

It was during that long-ago story time, I think, when I first knew I wanted to write a chapter book. I wanted to give other readers that experience I had treasured, so one day they might come back to my book and say, "Where were we?"

"What greater gift than the love of a cat?"

~ Charles Dickens

1

CHAPTER ONE

The World Outside the Window

Any cat lover will tell you there's no such thing as an ordinary cat. Cats themselves know this better than anyone. It shows in that regal way they carry themselves. So just because Rufus felt in his very bones that he was somehow *exceptional,* that didn't make him arrogant. It merely made him a cat.

All the same, exceptional was not the word Mama Cat would have used. *Different* was more like it, but... that wasn't quite it either. The exact word simply wouldn't come to her.

From dawn to dusk, her five other kittens tumbled and cavorted themselves into an exhausted heap of fur, but Rufus had no interest in such nonsense. He spent hours staring out the window. What on earth was he looking for anyway?

One troubling possibility nibbled at Mama Cat's peace of mind. Every evening as twilight settled in, Uncle Oscar, the old tom that lived with them, would plunk himself down by the fire, regaling any kitten who'd listen with yarns about his early days aboard a fishing trawler. He always began the same way: "Have I told you catlings 'bout the time I dang near died at sea?"

There were multiple versions of Oscar's hair-raising tango with death, and the kittens had heard them all—countless times. They didn't care. They couldn't get enough of Uncle Oscar dodging shivers of jagged-toothed sharks, wrangling grisly squid as they trussed him in tentacles long and thick as a ship's mast, or standing watch in the crow's nest while an epic storm swallowed islands whole. "After that storm, we had nothing t' eat for weeks," he'd tell them, "save cockroaches big as you catlings and meaner 'n a cornered rat."

Mama Cat herself didn't believe one word of this balderdash. But maybe, just maybe, tales invoking mythical beasts could make sea life wickedly enticing to a naïve kitten.

"Daydreaming about your destiny?" she asked Rufus one morning, working her rough tongue over the little sentry's thick fur.

The magical word awakened something in Rufus. "Destiny? What's that?" he inquired.

"Destiny, my darling," she replied, placing a firm paw over her squirming kit and drawing him close, "is the life you're born to live."

Rufus stopped fidgeting and looked up. "What's my destiny?" he asked, his heart pounding. He could almost hear the words forming in her head. Like Uncle Oscar, Rufus would sail the world, trouncing rogues and hooligans, weathering storms that could test the grittiest cat's mettle.

To his dismay, Mama Cat said nothing of the kind. "I'm afraid it's too early to say," was her evasive reply. "Destiny has a way of revealing itself when the time is right."

"The time is right now," Rufus insisted. If only Mama Cat would stop speaking in riddles for once and rain down some of that wisdom she kept doling out in bits and jots.

Mama Cat paused to gather her thoughts. She could see Rufus gazing over at Uncle Oscar with unmitigated affection. The big gray tom was dozing for the moment. Thank heavens. She was worn to tatters competing with that scallywag for her kittens' attention.

"Your destiny is part of you," she said at last, thinking how this precocious kit was never happy with the simple answer to anything. "Your spirit, your dreams, your very breath and blood. But destiny is shaped by the roads you choose to follow. In life, choices are everything. Here now—let's get those ears."

Ears??!! Who cared about ears? If only Mama Cat would stick to the point, and stop fussing over dirt only she could see.

"I'm… clean… *enough!*" Rufus declared, wriggling free and hoisting himself to the top of the big steamer trunk. His mother didn't agree, but she had five more baths to give, and no time to chase a headstrong kitten, clean ears or not.

At that moment, out of nowhere, it popped up—the word that fit Rufus so precisely. Singular. She must remember to tell him later. Only…

…would there be a later? They would come for this one, the humans. Soon. Mama Cat could feel it. They always took her most cherished kits first, before she could remember to tell them all the important things that mothers mean to say. She would miss her wannabe voyager with his never-ending queries. More than any other kitten from this litter. Maybe more than any kitten ever. She watched him resume his lookout atop the trunk, wishing she could keep him with her a little longer, knowing she could not.

The antique trunk was unquestionably, Rufus thought, the finest place in the house. Its banded sides made climbing easy for a young cat with short legs. Better still, it sat directly under the room's only window, offering an unobstructed view of the giant birch. Standing on his hind feet, front paws resting on the sill, Rufus could watch a never-ending stream of birds take off and rebound.

Why, he wondered, was he cooped up indoors while these flighty beings were free to come and go all the live-long day? It wasn't fair.

Engrossed in a raucous clash between two jays, Rufus never heard the approaching footsteps behind him, or the excited whispers coming closer... and closer still. Without warning, he was scooped up by hands that smelled of lavender soap and garden mulch, deposited in a basket normally used for cut flowers, and taken to a home with a forest on one side, a patch of wild iris on the other, and an earthen trail running up the middle.

The kitten with a destiny had landed right where he'd always wanted to be: in the world outside the window.

2

CHAPTER TWO

King of the Forest

That first night, Rufus missed his family, missed their warmth and the reassuring closeness of the small bed they'd shared. Luckily, his new companion, Mrs. Lin, knew a thing or two about loneliness.

She sat in her rocker by the fire, holding little Rufus on her lap, stroking him behind the ears in that very spot where his mother had always nuzzled him so tenderly, and singing her favorite song, "Moon River." It was the first time Rufus had heard anyone sing. The haunting melody touched something deep within him, and though he could make no sense of the lyrics, he knew he was listening to someone's heartfelt story. It was the first of many nights he would fall asleep this way.

On most mornings, Mrs. Lin woke before Rufus. "Will you look at that sunrise?" she would say, as if it were the first sunrise she had ever seen. She'd don her blue apron, smiling as Rufus stretched the sleep from his body. "You're thinking we should bake something, aren't you?" she'd ask. "Muffins? Popovers? Ah, you're right. Scones are just the ticket for a fine morning like this."

Rufus quickly understood that his role in baking was to keep an eye on Mrs. Lin, making sure she didn't forget important ingredients like salt or vanilla. And of course, to stroll past the oven now and again, checking for warmth. As the days went on, Rufus became something of a culinary prodigy, but cooking wasn't his only area of expertise.

In no time, he knew quite a lot about gardening as well. It was his favorite of their activities together because it took them where Rufus always longed to be: outdoors. The main purpose of gardening, Rufus gathered, was to dig holes in the flower bed's soft earth, something Mrs. Lin did with such art and panache one would almost think she had learned her technique from a cat. As always, she included Rufus in every step.

"Do we have enough lilies?" she would ask. As anyone could plainly see from his expression, Rufus didn't believe having enough lilies was even possible. "So—we need to add a clump or two then," Mrs. Lin would concede. "About here? Another fern as well? Brilliant. Why didn't I think of that?"

Rufus kept Mrs. Lin so busy planting that she must have felt grateful when he set off on his own to explore. The forest was alive with creatures, and creeping through it, Rufus felt that thrill that comes with being an undisputed sovereign. Birds erupted into flight at his approach, squirrels spiraled up trees, mice and chipmunks raced for the wood pile. It was good to be a cat.

Weeks flew by. Then months. Spring warmed into summer, which cooled into a crisp fall and mild winter now feeling its way into spring again.

By his first birthday, Rufus knew every lair and dogleg of the forest and iris patch. He'd climbed every standing tree, dwarf to giant, and paraded like a king down each fallen log. He knew where chickadees and robins nested, where voles and their ground squirrel cousins burrowed, where sun warmed the earth on chilly days, and where verdant ferns offered relief from summer's suffocating heat. It seemed he'd mastered everything his surroundings had to teach, and the perimeters of his new domain, once boundless as the sky, began closing in on him.

He recalled something Uncle Oscar had once said. "When your world grows too small, catling, you're the only one can make it bigger." He was itching to do that very thing. But how?

One sun-drenched morning, Rufus was helping Mrs. Lin plant violets, inhaling the pungent smell of peat moss, when a shrill cry jolted him from his reverie. He looked up in time to see a red-tailed hawk soaring overhead, bound for the wetlands or whatever lay beyond. Rufus realized he didn't even know what that something was, and would very much like to find out. It never occurred to the young king that he might be totally unprepared for such a journey.

3

CHAPTER THREE

Second Thoughts

Rufus decided to share his plan—which wasn't really a plan so much as an impulse—with Sadie and Karma, the silver-tipped Persians who lived next door. He needed to choose his words with utmost care, he told himself. Certainly, he had to appear dare devilish enough to pique their interest. Yet he couldn't make this scheme of his too tantalizing or the normally cautious Persians might demand to go along. And he couldn't have that. Could he?

As it turned out, all his shilly-shallying was for nothing. Sadie had no intention of taking part in such an insane escapade. "Why would I? Why would anyone?" she asked, shocked that Rufus would propose something so outrageous.

"Danger lurks everywhere," she went on, lifting an elegant paw for grooming. "Owls love to feast on cats and you'll never hear them coming. Behind every rock and shrub you'll find coyotes, raccoons, and the nastiest dogs anyone could dream up. Humans aren't always kind, either." She placed the finished foot beneath her and raised another, adding, "Even if you don't get eaten, you need to feed yourself. Dinner doesn't come to you in a dish, you know. Not in the wild. You have to hunt for it. You have to *kill* things—and some bite back." Lowering the second foot, Sadie leaned in close to Rufus, her warm breath caressing his face. "How do you feel about eating frogs and lizards... or *rats?*"

Rufus felt an icy finger of doubt touch his heart. What did he know of the world beyond the iris bed? What if he got lost? What if he died?

As these dark thoughts circled through his mind, Sadie, having made her point, rose to leave. The ever-silent Karma rose with her, and their silky fur entwined so beautifully it was impossible to tell where one cat left off and the other began.

Rufus watched in glum silence as the Persians padded toward the porch, heads touching as if they were sharing a secret. Which no doubt they were. Rufus wished he could listen in, but perhaps it was just as well he couldn't. Sadie was likely weighing the red cat's chances of surviving this wacky walkabout, and really, who needs to dwell on such things?

Then it occurred to him. He'd heard many a bloodcurdling tale from Uncle Oscar during those long nights by the fire. Mama Cat had never been convinced those stories held a single grain of truth—and even if they did, Uncle Oscar had come home without losing so much as one gray whisker. Sadie was toying with him. Concocting nightmares out of moon dust to frighten Rufus into staying put. Was he going to let her get by with that?

"Wait!" he cried. "How do you know all this? Have you been out there?"

It was too late. The silver cats were already far up the path, and Rufus's voice was lost in the whistle of a tall wind. He sat for a moment, mulling over Sadie's words. Maybe it was better to stay where he felt safe. Still… the thought of giving up on this new venture made him so gloomy he didn't know if he could bear it.

4

CHAPTER FOUR

Ain't Ya Curious?

She could have had any kitten in the litter, yet without a moment's hesitation Mrs. Lin had chosen Rufus. Was it the red fur and green eyes? Who can say?

From a cat's point of view, of course, appearance is of no concern. One human is much like another in that regard. Not that cats don't have preferences. They like gentle hands, mellow voices, and above all, well-prepared food. Mrs. Lin had a voice that could charm songbirds, and the loving touch that comes from years of tending delicate ferns and flowers. Better still, she could turn any fare from roast chicken to baked salmon—even canned sardines— into a banquet.

"Rufie darling, what do you fancy tonight?" she asked that evening, and without waiting for a reply, dropped some delectable tidbits of grilled trout into his dish.

Rufus barely looked up. Distracted by Sadie's warnings, he couldn't muster an appetite, despite the savory aromas filling the kitchen. It was time to make a choice: go or stay.

Leaving his food untouched, he gave Mrs. Lin that look that meant "Let me out. Please." Before the gardener could even finish opening the door, he had squeezed through.

Making his way to the edge of the yard, Rufus tipped back his head and drank in the night. The purple shadows were longer and deeper now. Shades of copper, rose, and gold splashed across a sky preparing to reveal its first stars, and the vastness of it made him feel anything was possible.

As he looked over his shoulder, Rufus noticed Sadie and Karma sitting on their porch as usual, watching him expectantly. He could guess what they were thinking. They didn't believe for one moment that he would leave the safety of the home and yard he'd come to know so well and head off into who knows what. No one, surely, would be so foolish.

Cool evening air drifted in from the wetlands, sweeping away the warmth of the day, ruffling the fur along Rufus's back. Through the open kitchen window, he could hear Mrs. Lin singing, her fluid voice streaming through the trees. He almost turned around at that point. Almost.

Then, in the stillness of twilight, he felt the steady beat of his heart, and knew that no matter what Sadie had said, he would be as brave as he needed to be. Uncle Oscar wouldn't be standing here all aquiver, letting doubts worm their way into his head, allowing someone else's misgivings to ruin his good times. "Hey, my young catling," he would whisper, "Whadya say we go see what's waiting past that far off bend? Ain't ya curious?"

He most certainly was curious. And hadn't Mama Cat always said that curiosity was the mark of a nimble mind? He had to know. *Was the world as thrilling as Uncle Oscar had made out? Or as fraught with danger as Sadie had painted it?* There was but one way to find out. Flicking his tail, he trotted past the iris bed and down the earthen path where he had never gone before, forcing himself not to look back.

5

CHAPTER FIVE

Out Where the Stories Are

From far beyond the forest, beyond the iris patch, a pond he'd never seen beckoned Rufus with an irresistible potpourri of scents: fish, frogs, cattails, blackbirds, old nests, mud, rotting leaves, goose droppings… and *mice.* He breathed it all in, his head awhirl. He could not have turned back now if he'd wanted to.

Home was soon far from sight, yet Rufus felt fairly sure of himself on the trail. And had he stuck to that well-trodden path—as he'd originally planned—everything might have gone differently. But that is rarely how life unfolds.

Gradually, the familiar wooded landscape transformed into a patchwork of meadows and wetlands. Carpets of purple asters and yellow marsh marigolds rolled out in all directions as the sun spilled the last of its light across the water and littoral mud

flats. Frogs began their nightly chorus. Dragonflies hovered and zoomed over the pond's glassy surface, and butterflies paused to drink from tiny rock pools. The world was reaching out its arms, enveloping the young swashbuckler in its embrace. Rufus was lulled into a sleepy tranquility until… like some skulking sea monster, Sadie's voice rose from the depths of his mind.

"Roooooo-fus, eyes are watching you," the voice taunted. "It will soon be dark… innnnnky dark. With nooooowhere to hide…"

"Hold on one bloomin' minute!" Uncle Oscar's gruff baritone cut in. "Are you really gonna listen to that fraidy-cat who's never budged off 'er own front porch?" The Oscar-y voice dropped to a throaty whisper. "Out there where you've never been, catling… that's where the stories are."

Surrendering to the spell of the old sailor's words, Rufus slipped into the underbrush with that cool composure only a cat can feel. The reeds grew taller, closing over Rufus's head, and Sadie's infernal buzzing was drowned in a rising symphony of frogs and crickets.

Though he had no way of knowing it, every step Rufus took brought him closer to the hideaway of two Canada geese. These resilient flyers had covered nearly fifteen hundred miles to reach their annual nesting site, a thinly veiled clearing near the pond's edge. After two days of collecting the right makings, the pair had put the finishing touches on their loosely woven nest of twigs and grass, lined it with moss and their own soft down, and filled it with a clutch of speckled eggs.

Now, as Rufus picked his way through the dense thicket of cattails, the geese found themselves awash in the dreaded stench of cat. With eggs to protect, neither was of a mind to humor some upstart feline. They braced for a fight.

Rufus also smelled the geese, but the scent was new to him, so he was more inquisitive than afraid. He poked his head between the stalks, seeking a better view, and was instantly deafened by the raspy trumpet of a female goose, bill open, tongue wagging furiously, eyes ablaze. The gander, who'd been guarding the female and her nest, stretched his neck long and low in that menacing stance that signals no quarter, and charged Rufus, hissing in rage. Rufus shrank back in alarm, but he was too slow by far. Before he could grasp what was happening, the goose had fetched him three bone-crushing blows to the head.

The big cat yowled in protest and clamped his eyes shut, a distinct disadvantage in a close fight. Instantly, the gander—a seasoned scrapper who had faced down several raccoons and one very tenacious Labrador—sensed his opponent's fear, and took full advantage, pummeling Rufus with a bill stout as a hammer.

Frantic, Rufus twitched and darted every which way. But where was there to go? If only the geese would hush their nerve-shattering racket, he thought, maybe he could get his wits about him. The louder they grew, the less Rufus could think, and soon he couldn't even recall which direction the path lay. Battling fatigue and terror, he scrambled for footing in slick mud that was rapidly matting every inch of his fur, threatening to suck him under.

The male goose tasted victory. Fanning his sinewy wings, he yanked the cat up by the nape of the neck, shook him like a raggedy clump of swamp grass, and shoved him headfirst into murky pond water. Rufus could not breathe. He had no doubt of the big gander's intentions. As brackish liquid oozed into his throat, it dawned on Rufus that Sadie might be clairvoyant.

6

CHAPTER SIX

An Unforeseen Rescue

Shortly before all this commotion, on the other side of the pond, Mr. Peabody had been trying to write a poem, but the words wouldn't come, and the harder he tried, the more they refused to appear on the page. He'd gotten as far as *"It's funny how…"* but couldn't finish the line.

Exasperated, he decided to make some tea. While it was steeping, a disarmingly agile mouse somehow catapulted itself onto the highest kitchen shelf, where it perched, maddeningly out of reach, sprucing up its whiskers. Flicking at the mouse with a towel, Mr. Peabody managed to break two teacups. By the time he got the mess cleaned up, his tea had cooled and the mouse had taken off—along with the last shreds of Mr. Peabody's poetic thoughts. It was becoming an altogether vexing day.

"It's funny how... writing puts you in the mood to go walking," Mr. Peabody quipped, hoping some fresh air would clear his head. He tugged on his wool coat, snatched his barely working flashlight from the closet, and headed down to the pond to see how the geese were doing. He had been watching two in particular, for they were sheltering no more than a pine cone's pitch from the path. Not safe. Not safe at all. Mr. Peabody knew that a coyote was prowling along the pond's edge, for he had seen her tracks, an unmistakable straight line of prints no other animal makes.

As he neared the nesting site, such a ruckus was brewing that Mr. Peabody assumed his worst fears were coming true. The coyote had discovered the nest and was making short work of eggs, geese, or both. He quickened his pace, but the frenzied barking of the geese made him worry he would never get to them in time. What he would do when faced with a full-grown coyote he had not the slightest idea, but confident he would think of something, he did not hesitate.

Shoving reeds and cattails aside, Mr. Peabody cast his fading light across the churned-up earth, and was astonished to see that the cause of all this hullabaloo was not a coyote at all. It appeared to be a cat—a rather mud-encrusted one at that—and he was clearly getting the worst of things. Far from being endangered, the geese were launching a full-fledged attack, and had nearly succeeded in drowning their intruder. They saw Mr. Peabody as one more annoyance in an already stressful evening, and forsaking Rufus for the moment, turned their attention to this two-legged nuisance, jabbing his ankles and tearing at his coat.

When Rufus felt the big gander release his grip, he wasted no time. Wheezing uncontrollably, he launched himself into the arms of his surprised rescuer, who jumped back, startled, leaving the geese to count their eggs and complain as loudly as if they had been the victims in this brouhaha.

Mr. Peabody had never held a cat before. This one looked and felt more like a soggy otter and smelled decidedly swampy.

"Who in the world might you be—and whatever made you decide to swim with the geese?" Mr. Peabody asked, glancing about hopefully for a place to set Rufus down. Meanwhile, Rufus sank his claws deep into the poet's coat to guarantee he could do no such thing.

"Something tells me you'd prefer to stay where you are," Mr. Peabody observed. "Probably a wise choice. If it's all the same to you then, I vote we leave these cantankerous characters to themselves."

Holding Rufus gingerly, the poet began retracing his steps, wondering whether his flashlight had a flicker of life remaining, whether his coat would ever smell like a coat again, and whether there was even the slightest chance that cats enjoyed baths.

7

CHAPTER SEVEN

Read the Eyes

From the moment he entered the poet's house, Rufus felt serene and content. The place smelled of wood smoke, lemon verbena, herbal tea—and books. Hundreds of them. The lights were dim and cozy, the furniture worn to a luxuriant softness. He loved the wide plank floors with their foot friendly rag rugs, the black wood stove with its tea kettle simmering away, and most of all, the expansive window sills just made for a cat who liked overseeing the day's events. It was almost as if he'd been born right here and had finally returned home.

Rufus followed Mr. Peabody to a mud room off the back porch, where a mica-shaded lamp layered everything in its rich amber glow. Stretched along one wall was a wooden workbench with a deep sink. Towels, soaps, and brushes occupied nearby shelves.

Mr. Peabody slung his spattered coat over a wooden chair, carefully boosted Rufus onto the workbench, and began running water into a silver washtub—testing with his fingers until the temperature was just so. The way he liked his own baths. "Perfect," he assured Rufus, smiling into the big green eyes that never left his own.

Now came the moment he'd fretted over the whole way home—lifting the cat into the tub. Mr. Peabody knew that the best way to inspire trust is to act as if you know what you are doing, even if you do not. "Easy now—that's the way," he said, aware that he was mostly talking to himself as he picked Rufus up with strong hands.

To Mr. Peabody's relief, Rufus sank into the soothing warmth without objection, blissfully closing his eyes and stirring the water with his tail. Once he'd rinsed off every hint of muck and mire, Mr. Peabody bundled his guest in a large yellow towel, patting him lightly, being as careful of paws and ears as if he dried waterlogged cats every day of his life. When the towel had soaked up every drop it could hold, he gathered it into a soggy bundle, unmasking Rufus. The emerging color of the cat's fur took the poet's breath away. "Will you look at that . . ." he whispered. "Never underestimate the power of a good bath."

Mr. Peabody made Rufus a bed out of a feather pillow encircled by the softest flannel shirts. Only someone who has slept in such a bed can fathom how exquisitely welcoming it is. After a thoughtful turn or two, Rufus settled in and began licking himself back into shape.

Meanwhile, his host returned to the kitchen. Bath time had gone better than he'd feared it might. But now he faced another quandary: what to feed his guest.

He needn't have worried. It turned out the two friends shared an affinity for crab cakes, which Mr. Peabody—a much better cook than he gave himself credit for—fried up to a golden loveliness. As he was turning the cakes, the poet felt something brush his

leg, and looked down to see that Rufus was now nearly twice his previous size, his long auburn hair fluffy as a lion's mane.

They dined to their hearts' content, Rufus seated at the table, eating from a blue plate identical to Mr. Peabody's. Rufus ate without looking up. His companion, however, who'd had no one to talk to in months, barely drew breath, going on about the rudeness of geese and the frustration of writing poems when the words you needed seemed to have gone on holiday.

After dinner, both slept soundly, Rufus in his feather bed, the poet beneath his forest green down comforter. Through the night, Mr. Peabody never stirred. But sometime before dawn, Rufus climbed onto the window sill, recalling a night from long ago when he and Mama Cat had watched the stars together, the two of them alone in an expanding universe. Mama Cat had revealed something Rufus found wondrous—but unsettling. He'd soon find himself, she said, in a world where humans outnumbered cats.

"Read the eyes, my little one," she'd told Rufus. "The eyes will always tell you which humans, or cats, to trust."

The same might be said for geese, Rufus thought.

8

CHAPTER EIGHT

Cat Person

The next morning, Mr. Peabody was sure that Rufus—dry, well-fed, and rested—would head out the front door for home. But that is not how things went. Not only did Rufus stay for a scrambled egg breakfast, but he stayed the rest of the day, and the day after that, and the one after that as well.

In less than a week's time, Rufus was following the poet about as if he knew the routine by heart, which soon enough he did. Mr. Peabody awoke each morning to the rhythm of Rufus kneading the down comforter, where the big cat liked to sleep on nights when thunder shook the windows or hail battered the roof. Rufus then followed Mr. Peabody to the kitchen, weaving in and out between two stocking covered legs as his host made toast and tea, and listening for that all-important question: "Mr. Cat, what do you say we play with words?"

When Mr. Peabody sat down at the kitchen table to write, Rufus made himself at home on the upper half of the paper, eyes half closed, purring along as Mr. Peabody hummed some song or other he hadn't thought of in years. And all the while, words and phrases poured into the poet's head so easily it seemed the poems were writing themselves.

Because cats are driven to investigate every nook of wherever they find themselves, it had taken Rufus only minutes to discover that Mr. Peabody's back yard was a climber's paradise. Whenever the big cat needed a break from the intensity of writing, a giant boulder lured him to its flat summit, where he had a panoramic view of the yard and neighboring field. Close by, a century-old oak with a mammoth trunk and capacious crown twisted up and up to dizzying heights like some fantastical mushroom. From its topmost branches, Rufus could see forever—beyond marshes and grasslands to the ocean inlet, and across its turquoise and sapphire waters to the horizon itself.

The two friends spent afternoons sharing the Adirondack chair on the front porch, where Mr. Peabody read his favorite poems aloud. Verses by Robert Frost, Billy Collins, or Nikki Giovanni. Sometimes e. e. cummings, Emily Dickinson, or Maya Angelou. Rufus would sprawl out on one of the chair's ample, weathered arms, dozing off to the pleasant drone of the poet's voice.

"Mr. Cat," his friend would say, as the two sensed dinner time approaching, "you have impeccable taste in poetry."

And in all this time, did Rufus ever miss his home with Mrs. Lin? He must have. But a heart that craves adventure will endure many things, even the poignant twinge of homesickness, to keep good times from winding down too soon.

As for Mr. Peabody, he was learning something about himself he'd never realized until now. He was a cat person. How he could have lived so long without knowing such a thing was a mystery, and he decided he rather liked this new side to himself.

9

CHAPTER NINE

Abandoned

Across the pond, a different scenario was playing out. Mrs. Lin's usually bright kitchen was dark and silent, the oven cold, the inviting aromas of fresh bread and scones long faded. The gardener couldn't work up the energy to sing these days. What good were songs with no one curling up by the fire to hear them?

In the garden, weeds flourished. Iris well past their prime wilted on pale green stalks, while bees and butterflies looked for nectar elsewhere. Ferns thirsted for water that never came. And black garden boots sat abandoned by a back door nobody had opened in ages.

Each morning, Mrs. Lin stood on her veranda, surveying the forest, meadows, and marshlands surrounding her cabin. Leaning over the railing, she could see almost to the edge of the pond, and she'd walked that far and then some, more than once, in search of her beloved friend. Where could he have gone?

The gardener tried unsuccessfully to extinguish her most troubling fantasies. What if some famished coyote had turned Rufus into brunch? Or some marauding eagle had carted him off into oblivion? What if he had drowned? Surely, he had not simply left, seeking a new home. That was a thought so painful Mrs. Lin found herself saying out loud, "No! That cannot be." She vowed she would never—not ever—give up looking. Not if she had to look for the rest of her life.

CHAPTER TEN

One Dreadful Tuesday

r. Peabody soon had enough poems to fill a book. On those few occasions when he wasn't writing, he experimented with recipes old and new, thoughtfully sampling the results from a wooden spoon, occasionally adding a smidgen of this, a pinch of that.

The kitchen window had blossomed into an herb garden boasting not only verbena, but also sage, basil, Rosemary, thyme, and naturally, catnip. The stove was always warm, hot tea only a quick pour away. Mr. Peabody had purchased a wicker basket into which he placed the feather pillow and flannel shirts of which his guest had become so fond.

It was deeply gratifying, the poet thought, to finally have someone with whom he could converse. "Where did I put my glasses, Mr. Cat?" he would ask, though they were usually resting on his head. Granted, Rufus didn't speak exactly, but he was the consummate listener, hanging on the poet's every word, seldom interrupting, never too busy to hear whatever Mr. Peabody was working on at the moment.

"Listen to this line, Mr. Cat," the poet said one evening as they sat together on the couch. *"It's funny how you go looking for one thing… and come home with a friend.* Do you like the sound of that? It ought to be among your favorites, for it's about you—and what's more, you helped write it, if you recall. I can see you're looking concerned, but yes, the poem will grow longer. They always do."

Perhaps nothing would have changed for years had Mr. Peabody not made a nightly habit of reading the paper. He did read it though, every word. And thus, far more swiftly than it had come together, this idyllic scene came unraveled.

One dreadful Tuesday evening, right on page 17 under "Pets," there appeared a photograph Mr. Peabody would have recognized anywhere, a face like no other. It was his very own Mr. Cat, and he had another name: Rufus.

What's more, he had another home, with someone named Mrs. Lin. She was *desperate* to have him back, and was imploring anyone who had seen him to please, *please* let her know.

Just like that, Mr. Peabody faced a terrible decision. He could hardly imagine going back to his life before Rufus, and for that reason, understood all too well how Mrs. Lin must miss her companion.

11

CHAPTER ELEVEN

The Wish

Anyone glancing through Mrs. Lin's kitchen window when she answered her phone the following afternoon would have known straightaway she was receiving welcome news. Her eyes shimmered and her mouth softened into a smile. Murmuring a heartfelt *Thank you,* she stepped outside, took her Red Flyer wagon by the handle, and headed for a house she'd passed numerous times but had never visited until now, her feet virtually dancing along the path.

When Mrs. Lin showed up at the door, Rufus greeted her as if she'd been stopping by every day. Though she knew he was not overly fond of hugs, the gardener couldn't help herself. "Rufie, dear heart, you look so... *loved,*" she breathed, clasping him a tad more zealously than she'd intended. Rufus put up with a cuddle or two, then thumped to the floor, where he commenced weaving figure eights around four familiar legs—two in striped stockings, two in black garden boots.

As they stood watching the big cat together, neither gardener nor poet could find an easy way to move things along. Mrs. Lin did not relish the thought of leaving Mr. Peabody alone, nor did he look forward to saying goodbye.

"I guess we cannot very well stand here forever," Mr. Peabody said at last. "Though if I could stop time at this moment, I believe I would."

In the end, it was Rufus who brought things to a head. He hopped into the wagon, curling his lavish tail beneath him, and was soon bumping along down the path with the gardener chatting away, whether to Rufus or simply to herself no one can say. Rufus watched as the poet grew smaller… and smaller still… finally vanishing from sight altogether.

Mr. Peabody waited until the wagon bearing his dear Mr. Cat disappeared round the wide bend just shy of the cattails. He then turned and went into the house, but when he got inside, he could not recall why he was there. Feeling as if he'd been set adrift on an ice floe, he came back out and slumped onto the step, gazing out at nothing in particular, waiting. Waiting for what, he wasn't sure. He scanned the sky, hoping for some sort of answer, and there it was, with uncanny timing. The first star.

He should make a wish, he supposed. Would it help? It couldn't hurt, he decided. The poet closed his eyes, searching in vain for words to quell the sea of despair rising around him. Though he would have given anything to have Rufus back, the memory of Mrs. Lin's happy face made those deep personal longings feel selfish. "If only," he sighed, "I could have someone wonderful to share crab cakes with again." As wishes go, that one seemed downright pathetic, but it was the best he could do at the moment.

12
CHAPTER TWELVE

Unbearable Silence

The next day, Mr. Peabody made tea as usual, but he forgot both lemon and sugar so it was barely drinkable. He forced himself to sit at the kitchen table, where he'd always done his best writing, but the poems that drizzled from his pen were sad and moody, and he wound up crossing out almost every word.

Several times he opened the kitchen cupboard only to stand there baffled, wondering when or why he'd purchased such useless items. What did it matter? Food wasn't the answer.

Everywhere he looked he could see Rufus—preening, dozing, basking in the sun. A dozen times he heard the cat outside, begging to be let in, but when he sprang to his feet and swung the door wide, Rufus was never there.

That night, he missed Rufus's pulsating purr and the weight of the cat's round, solid body warming his knobby old knees through the comforter. When morning came, Mr. Peabody was not sure whether he had ever closed his eyes.

What he did know for certain was that he could not stay in this silent house one moment longer. Without taking time for breakfast or tea, he grabbed his coat, forgetting his hat, and set out across the meadow, a determined look on his face.

13

CHAPTER THIRTEEN

You Can Always Say No

The breeze was blustery, and since Mr. Peabody had the sort of hair that could barely stay put even in calm weather, he resembled a dandelion puff ball by the time he arrived at his destination. Mrs. Lin had to stifle a laugh as she opened the door to welcome him: "My dear friend, come in out of that wind! I'm baking cookies, and you're just in time for a taste."

Scents of chocolate, brown sugar, and buttery pecans swirled through Mrs. Lin's wood-beamed kitchen. Sampling cookies was one of Mr. Peabody's specialties, and since he almost never made them for himself, this was an unexpected treat. As he hung his coat by the door, however, a single question burned through his mind: "Where is he?" Had he said those words aloud or merely thought them?

"He'll be along," Mrs. Lin said, pulling a steaming batch of cookies from the oven and sliding several onto a plate. "But I have something to show you—something I think you'll find incredibly interesting."

Mr. Peabody couldn't conceive of anything half so interesting as seeing Rufus again, but he forced himself to be polite. Pulling up to the kitchen table, he reached for a cookie. Before he could take a bite, Mrs. Lin shoved a page from the newspaper in front of him. "Look," she said. "Just *look*—and she needs a home."

Under "Pets," right in the spot where Rufus's picture had been a few days ago, was a new picture. A cat far leaner than Rufus, with longer legs and bigger feet, thick-as-a-rug black fur and fierce blue eyes. At least they *looked* blue, but it can be hard to tell such things from a newspaper photo. She had unusual ears—or perhaps part of that left one was missing. The blurb in the paper said she was a stray, up for adoption, and needed "a loving home" for she had an "independent personality."

Absent-mindedly nibbling his cookie, Mr. Peabody examined the photo.

"Well? What do you think?" Mrs. Lin asked.

"Ah, very good. *Extremely* good," Mr. Peabody replied, smiling up at Mrs. Lin's inquiring face. "I could eat the whole batch!"

"No—I mean about *this*," Mrs. Lin said, tapping the photo with her finger.

Mr. Peabody took another bite and continued chewing, his eyes reluctantly returning to the newspaper. He didn't know *what* he thought, really. He knew he missed Rufus more than he'd ever missed anyone or anything. Earlier, he'd had some wild idea that perhaps Mrs. Lin would see how forlorn he felt without his soulmate, and just say that the big red cat could go home with him. Now he realized how ridiculous that had been. Perhaps he could come to see Rufus now and then, but that too seemed absurd—walking a mile to visit a cat. Did anyone *do* that?

"I think we should go get her," Mrs. Lin was saying.

Mr. Peabody continued to study the photo. He'd already adopted one cat out of the blue, and then lost him. Now Mrs. Lin was trying to talk him into another. When she said *"We* should go get her," she really meant that *he* should go get her. It sounded like a spectacularly loony idea. This cat was not beautiful like Rufus. She looked as if she'd been in fights. What if she liked to bite? Or scratch?

Mrs. Lin persisted. "It won't hurt to go *look* at her. She can't stay at the shelter forever. And *you* need a cat. You can always say no."

14
CHAPTER FOURTEEN

Phooey on Wishes

The truth is, you cannot always say no. Sometimes, it is very hard. Perhaps it was Mrs. Lin's relentless enthusiasm, or the cavernous hole in Mr. Peabody's heart. Or maybe it was the way this know-it-all cat sashayed up to him as if she were picking him out, not the other way around.

Before Mr. Peabody could talk himself out of what he feared might be a mistake, he was bouncing home in Mrs. Lin's twenty-year-old Jeep, balancing a wooden box on his lap. A box originally used for shipping pears. Inside was a black one-eared cat, scrutinizing him with the most piercingly blue eyes Mr. Peabody had ever seen. In his mind, he had already named her Asha, which means "wish," thinking she might be the friend he had hoped for.

Somehow though, he wasn't a believer. Mr. Peabody knew

from experience that wishes hardly ever turn out as we expect. Doubts buzzed through his head, creating a frown that clung to his face the whole way home. It seemed best not to mention that he wasn't at all sure about this new cat, and might not keep her.

15

CHAPTER FIFTEEN

The Test

The black cat seemed young, judging by her quickness, though the shelter people had not known her precise age. Despite her lush coat, several scars were readily visible up close, and her partially severed ear gave her a lopsided look. Unlike Rufus, she was no lap cat. Yet she had approached Mr. Peabody as if she'd known him for years, and that sheer pluckiness had won him over. He could see now that he'd made a hasty decision.

Asha kept her distance at first, only occasionally allowing Mr. Peabody to touch her. She did not respond to the name he'd given her. Perhaps she was used to some other name—or didn't really see the point of names.

Apparently, she had no ear for poetry, either. Now and then, hoping to share a new line or verse, Mr. Peabody would say, "Lady

Asha, could you take a moment…" But before he could finish speaking, the black cat would be out the door, and he was left reading to himself.

To call her unpredictable was an understatement. She could wolf down a crab cake in three bites, but was just as likely to walk away as if she couldn't be bothered with something as mundane as dinner.

Keeping track of her was a challenge. Asha was here, there, and everywhere, vaulting onto the highest rafters, or compressing her lithe form into ridiculously cramped spaces—inside cupboards, behind cabinets, under a couch. She could hide in a rain boot or hat. A terra cotta pot. A shoebox or watering can.

She let herself in and out, and Mr. Peabody had no idea how until he came across a tear she'd ripped in the screen door. He patched it at once. She made another.

The poet began to get the idea that whether this free spirit stayed with him was much less his choice than hers. Then, something happened to bring them closer. Asha promptly dispatched the mouse Mr. Peabody had pursued for weeks—and two others he had not even known were living with him. The delight he expressed when she laid each mouse at his feet created a fragile bond.

After his elated acceptance of each mouse gift, Asha moved to the foot of Mr. Peabody's bed in an apparent gesture of friendship. Yet, for both of them, something was clearly missing. Asha seemed restless. And Mr. Peabody felt as if he were taking a test and not doing terribly well. On the one hand, it was good to have a cat in the house again, but the poet was coming to realize that one cat cannot replace another, any more than one friend can replace another.

16
CHAPTER SIXTEEN

Secrets

It was one of the first truly warm days of the young summer. Cattails were sprouting profusely, and the blackbirds warbled their approval. Lavender edged clouds sailed through azure skies, while butterflies swooped in to kiss the newly budded sage. The geese were preoccupied with their six goslings, all crackerjack swimmers, and swallows dipped and wheeled, chasing moths and mayflies.

Mrs. Lin fetched the wagon and placed a box of fresh cookies in the corner—along with two magnificent purple iris. "What's better than cookies and flowers?" she asked Rufus, who couldn't think of a thing, and leaped aboard, seeming to know where they were headed.

The tilt and sway of the wagon had nearly put Rufus to sleep by the time they pulled up in front of Mr. Peabody's house, where they spotted him sitting alone in his Adirondack chair. No books, no pen and paper, and no cat. As they approached, he jumped up, and with a shrug announced simply, "She's gone."

When it comes to cats, of course, gone often means out of sight—for the moment. Still, they might not have found Asha for days had Rufus not intervened. As if Asha were calling to him, Rufus bounded from the wagon and walked right to her.

Why hadn't Mr. Peabody noticed it before? The bottom drawer of the bedroom chest was open ever so slightly. Familiar blue eyes peered up at them from a cushy nest of winter socks, and the black cat wasn't alone. Between her paws was a minute ball of fur with no visible face, feet, or tail. Was it breathing? Hard to tell. *Another dead mouse,* was Mr. Peabody's first thought, so he was taken aback when Mrs. Lin let out a tender "Ooooh," and carefully reached down to stroke the silken body with one finger.

It hit Mr. Peabody then. This diminutive surprise was no mouse. It was Asha's first—and only—kitten. They named him Razi, which means "Little Secret."

"Can't believe there's just one," Mr. Peabody whispered. "Isn't that unusual?"

"Not for a cat that's known rough times," the gardener answered softly. "The good news is, this one is so… perfect."

When a kitten is around, especially a perfect kitten, it's difficult if not impossible to focus on anything else. Small wonder that neither poet nor gardener noticed the looks passing between Rufus and Asha.

Unlike humans, cats can read each other instantly. They don't need time, shared experience, or conversation. They are cats, and that is enough.

In one electrifying rush, Rufus discerned what Mr. Peabody had spent days working out. He was nose to nose with something primal. Unbridled as a north country river. Profoundly alive. The black cat smelled of pine and grass, fresh rain, spring earth. Rufus was drawn to her the way we are all drawn to the wilderness.

Asha's eyes burrowed into the red cat's very soul, where our hidden thoughts, our truest selves reside. Buried deep was that indomitable will that is every cat's legacy. But something more. This cat was unlike others. Insanely intuitive. Unwavering as the tide. Genuinely selfless. For a cat. She could trust him, she knew, to guard her secrets, her life—and her blood.

Beneath her, Asha could feel Razi's heartbeat quicken, and she slowed her breathing until his slowed to match. He nudged her, moving close, seeking milk and warmth. This wild offspring, her little kit, her only kit, would have a life different from the hard one she'd lived. Instinct had brought her to the right place.

17
CHAPTER SEVENTEEN

Ready or Not

Despite his unimposing size, Razi was game as any tiger, and within weeks was racing Rufus to the top of the big rock, and storming up the hundred-year-old oak, hazarding onto limbs too frail even for his slight weight. He seemed unbothered when the flimsy branches gave way, dumping him onto a sturdier perch below.

Mr. Peabody was infatuated with Razi, and took such good care of him that he often forgot to feed Asha. She didn't mind. An empty dish gave her an opportunity to show Razi how to scavenge for the kind of food humans don't usually provide.

While Rufus looked on from the shadows, Asha taught Razi to crouch motionless, wait for the slightest shimmer in the long grass, then pounce on whatever might be hiding there. They

stalked grasshoppers, moths, and beetles first, lizards and tree frogs next, and finally mice and voles. The voles were particularly wily, but after a few skirmishes, proved themselves no match for Razi's sly maneuvers and lightning strikes.

"He's nearly ready," Asha told Rufus one day, as they reclined on the big rock that had become their special place.

Arching his back, Rufus stretched his legs to their full length, soaking in the heat of sun baked granite and watching Razi steal within inches of a hopping sparrow. "Ready for what?" he yawned.

"For me to go," Asha said.

Rufus went numb. Though he'd known Asha only a short while, it seemed they'd been friends forever. He'd promised himself that if Asha ever left, he would go too. That day had always seemed far in the future. Until suddenly, it wasn't.

18

CHAPTER EIGHTEEN

The Hardest Thing

Feeling the life drain from his body, Rufus struggled to stand.

"I'm coming with you," he said, the words out before he could stop them. Had he lost his mind?

Asha, fortunately, had other ideas.

"That wouldn't be wise," she said gently.

"Why? I can keep up!" he said, wondering what sort of madcap claim he thought he was making. While he'd learned a great deal about hunting in recent weeks, Rufus still liked the thought of crab cakes or sardines waiting on his plate at the end of the day.

"Even if you could," Asha said, "think how cold this world would be without you to warm it. No one will miss me."

"I will miss you!" Rufus protested. "This is your home!"

Asha looked around thoughtfully.

"You're right. Home is partly a place, but mostly I think . . . it's a feeling," she said at last. "I've lived in barns and attics, on an old fishing boat, in a deserted carnival, under a railroad car, and once, before I knew better, in a coyote's abandoned cave. Not one of those places felt like home. Maybe because I always had to fight for a dry corner to sleep in.

"I've fought snakes, snarling dogs, starving cats, and rats as big as you..."

She paused a moment to rub a paw over her nicked ear. "I chose this place for Razi, not for me. The poet is a good person. That's why I picked him, same as you did. I never meant to stay."

Rufus stared at her. "I didn't *pick* him," he countered. "He rescued me."

Asha was silent for a moment, cocking her head. "I'm pretty sure you rescued each other," she said. "You touch hearts, my red-haired friend. It's your destiny."

Destiny! Rufus hadn't thought of that word in months. What did any of this have to do with destiny? "Destiny," he cried, "is about . . . discovering who we're meant to be."

Asha crinkled her eyes, a cat's way of smiling. "We're meant to be explorers," she said, "Every one of us. It's the first thing we learn, essential as breathing.

"Over time, though, we become many things. You have a gift, Rufus. You heal the cracks and chasms life leaves behind, making everyone around you feel . . . whole again. Mended. I can teach Razi all there is to know about being a cat. You are showing him something I cannot. How to be a friend. The humans will love him for that, you know—and it will make all the difference."

Rufus looked dumbfounded. And Asha realized then that the red cat didn't yet fully understand the hold he had on humans. He would. In time.

"Aren't you teaching him the most important thing of all?" Rufus asked softly. "To be fearless?"

Asha looked deep into those green eyes. "No one is fearless," she said. "Without fear, we might never become who we need to be. Bravery is nothing more than pushing through your fear to reach what matters.

"Besides," she continued, "you're forgetting how much courage it takes to love someone. Friends don't always love us back. Sometimes they hurt us, even when they don't mean to." She paused. "Or leave us. Friendship is the most daring thing we ever attempt."

Rufus looked at her in disbelief. "Being someone's friend is easy."

"Only you would think that," said Asha. "For most of us, it's the hardest thing there is. We spend our whole lives learning to do it."

Her words stunned Rufus. He'd always looked up to Asha. Now she was talking as if he were some kind of hero. He collapsed onto the rock, feeling about as heroic as a leaf in a storm, and wishing the wind would carry him over fields and treetops and into tomorrow. Asha was leaving, and he couldn't do one thing to stop it. Maybe being a friend was hard after all—at least when it came time to say goodbye. He'd never thought of it that way until now. Why would he? He'd always been the one to go.

19

CHAPTER NINETEEN

No Second Chance

*R*ufus told himself he would remain awake for days if that's what it took. If Asha wouldn't take him with her, he'd follow at a distance to see where she was headed.

Asha knew all too well what the red cat was up to, and what she must do to keep him safe. It would take patience. A skilled hunter, she had plenty of that. Through the night, though Rufus was unaware of it, she watched him tirelessly. Waiting. As the last stars began to fade, Rufus could no longer keep his eyelids from drooping. It was time.

Silent as the dawn itself, Asha slid through the new opening in the screen door. Mr. Peabody was slumbering peacefully, Razi curled on top of his feet. Neither saw or heard a thing.

Someone else was watching, though. A young female golden eagle who routinely patrolled the wetlands had waited for this moment—and she was trouble. An assassin.

As Asha stole through the whispering grasses, the raptor spiraled lower, gauging her odds of success. Riding thermals on six feet of winged power, the golden was all but invisible against the gauzy pre-dawn sky. Her lethal talons were infused with a grip eight times that of the strongest human, her eyesight keen enough to spot a trembling mouse from a thousand feet up.

Still, nothing was certain. Even if she swept in low, a strike would be difficult—and dicey. Fishing had not been good of late, and the eagle could not afford another miss. A well-fed cat would keep her chicks warm and full for several days. This cat was nearly as big as she was, though, and carrying her to a nest atop the tallest snag in the forest would take every ounce of strength the eagle had. What's more, the black cat was fast. Faster than most. There would be no room for mistakes. And no second chance.

Asha had been hunted by many a skillful predator—foxes, coyotes, owls, even hawks. Never an eagle, though. Until now. This was a treacherous game.

Keeping the big oak between herself and the raptor, Asha scaled the trunk effortlessly, easing onto a gnarled branch that overhung the fence. Her eyes traced the eagle's every arc and roll. Her belly skimming the bark, Asha sidled down the length of the heavy bough, pausing where the leaves thinned, her dark form still camouflaged beneath their shimmering canopy. As she watched, the sun pushed over the distant hills, flooding the sky with light. And voila. The assassin was gone. *Where?*

With surreal calm, the cat gathered her legs beneath her, eyeing the wild blackberries just feet away. Forming a dense mat, the thorny shrubs hugged the hills beyond Mr. Peabody's yard for more than a mile, thinning near the ocean inlet. Deep within that tangled foliage, Asha had discovered a little-known tunnel carved

in some distant time by weasels, and through that escape route she could move undetected. If she could get there.

Survival hinged on speed and timing. She would need to move as never before. She would need to fly.

From nowhere, the winged predator reappeared. She hung there in the sky, suspended, motionless, deadly... then, in a cunning attempt to flush her prey, dove for earth with blinding velocity.

Asha held her breath, still as stone, her body a coiled spring.

Like some manic boomerang, the eagle pulled from her dive and soared for the light.

As the raptor was devoured by the sun, the cat exploded from the tree, her feet already digging for turf.

20

CHAPTER TWENTY

Gifts Left Behind

In the days following Asha's departure, Rufus was beside himself. His heavy heart repeatedly led him down the well-known path to visit Razi and Mr. Peabody, whose joy at seeing his old writing cohort shone in his eyes like sun on water.

Having two homes felt as natural to Rufus now as having two front feet. What he could not get used to was life without Asha. More than once, he was overcome by an urge to track her. Could he do that without getting lost? He wasn't sure. Could he make it back alive? Not a chance.

Rufus spent hours on the big rock, pondering his shadow as if to make Asha's reappear beside it. He climbed the giant oak higher than ever before, scouring the horizon, but finding not the slightest trace of cat. Only a lone eagle, circling endlessly.

Asha had been right that friendship was risky. His feelings were proof. But that wasn't the whole truth. Friends could also sing you to sleep when you ached for your mother's touch, pluck you from some fetid swamp and carry you home for crab cakes, or fill your life with things you would come to love. Poetry. Songs. The warmth of a wood stove.

True, Asha had left Rufus desolate, but she'd also given him a priceless gift: freedom. He knew how to keep an eye out for hawks and owls, avoid the coyote's trail, and melt into the brush and tall grasses where predators couldn't get to him.

As the weeks went by, he began to relish his treks through the outback, and learned that recounting his exploits to Sadie and Karma was a dandy antidote for the melancholy he feared might do him in. Having learned a thing or two from Uncle Oscar, Rufus didn't hesitate to season his stories with a hefty dose of imagination.

"Have I told you two about the time I nearly drowned?" he'd ask. The Persians would look unimpressed—at first—but their widening eyes gave the red cat the kind of encouragement a good raconteur lives for.

"I was bushwhacked by a horde of vampire geese," Rufus would continue. "Two bloodthirsty killers dragged me under by the ears while three murderous cutthroats latched onto my tail like pirates filching treasure."

Sadie would later whisper to Karma that the geese seemed to grow larger, more barbaric, and more numerous with every telling. Karma didn't disagree. But Razi, who'd heard this tale since birth, thought the geese were barely getting ghoulish enough to be interesting.

One might think Razi would have missed Asha more than anyone else, but truth be told, he was too busy making himself irreplaceable, something at which cats excel. He'd picked up all the ways and wiles a young cat needs to get along, and now spent his days helping Mr. Peabody compose poetry, keeping the house and garden free of pests, and practicing his hunting skills by ambushing Rufus, who good-naturedly endured the young cat's stealth attacks.

"Catling," Rufus would tell the blue-eyed assailant, "I could see you coming from clear back by the big rock." That wasn't even remotely true. Razi had benefited from a great teacher, and when it came to disguising his whereabouts, he was—except for the teacher herself—unrivaled. Still, Rufus resolved to keep the young cat on his toes. Asha would expect nothing less.

As for Mr. Peabody, it was nearly two days before he even noticed his shrewd black mouser was gone. It occurred to him that she might have gotten into trouble, but he doubted it. Asha could take care of herself. She was that sort of cat.

Meanwhile, he had the very thing he'd wished for: someone with whom to share crab cakes. Two someone's on nights when

Rufus stayed for dinner, and three when his favorite gardener dropped by with cookies, which seemed to be happening more and more often.

Mr. Peabody didn't really expect to see Asha again, but with cats, you never know. He kept an extra blue plate on the table just in case.

EPILOGUE

The Meaning of Home

The underside of the dock was damp most of the time, slick with algae and seaweed. It smelled of clams, dead fish, and barnacles that coated the slowly rotting wood. But in the remotest corner, in darkness too dense for any human eye to penetrate, was a high, dry spot sheltered from rain, wind, and waves. It was the kind of place that calls to a cat who has spent too long living on handouts and now craves food from the wild.

As fate would have it, that snug corner was currently home to a rogue rat who'd grown fat eating unwary crabs, fish hijacked when no one was watching, and discarded bait. The scruffy rodent both smelled and heard the cat coming, and emitted an angry hiss, baring his long yellow teeth. He'd scrapped ruthlessly to take over this hidey-hole, and had no intention of giving it up.

He was a veteran, an aging rat who mostly kept to himself these days. His battle-scarred face had persuaded many a cat to seek cover elsewhere. He wasn't about to back down for this one, the gritty, despicable pest he'd never been able to bully—not even when he'd moved in close enough to nip off part of her left ear. If things went his way, he'd get the rest of that ear today, and the other one as well. He blinked his lifeless eyes and waited.

Then… there she was. Back.

She skated under the dock with ethereal grace, edging over the struts, calculating every step like a tightrope walker. In the blink of an eye she was looking down on the hoary rodent from the topmost rafter. He didn't like that, and let out a gravelly snarl to show his displeasure.

Deliberately, soundlessly, the cat inched ever closer, hunkering low, keeping her good ear flattened to her head, her claws extended, her blue eyes locking onto the rat's steely glare. She was sleeker, heavier—and nervier—than she'd been in their old days together. She'd been eating well, that was certain, but it hadn't curbed her knack for the hunt.

A lifetime of pursuing prey and eluding predators guided the black cat to a strategic spot directly over the varmint's head, leaving his neck and back exposed—though well-guarded by those long teeth. Any moment, she might spring. Did she dare? The gleam in her eyes ignited. And for both of them, the time for bluffing was up.

She was far and away faster than memory had fooled him into believing, clipping inches off his scaly tail before he could even turn his head. His squeal swelled to an ear-splitting crescendo that screamed down the length of the dock. The pain would subside and his ravaged tail would heal, but his ego would never recover. For all his bravado, the rat had been lucky—and he knew it. Had she been of a mind, the black cat could have done far worse. He would need to scout out a new home now, and that was inconvenient. Especially in the rain.

The cat wasn't sorry to see her old nemesis skedaddle, his wrinkly toes shuffling over the timbers. The place smelled ratty, but that would fade with time. It still had that rugged cross beam that provided a secure harbor, even during high tides.

Asha tucked herself deep into her well-remembered corner, licking a long scratch that would soon turn into a scar. One of many. Was it the warmth of the dry wood? Maybe. For one nostalgic flash, Asha was back on the big granite rock, reliving her encounter with the surly rodent. What royal entertainment the red cat would spin from such a tale. He was with her in that corner for a second. She could feel his presence. Friend. Story teller. Mender of hearts.

Asha's coat would never fully cover her new welt, just as the tip of her damaged ear would never grow back. Before those prickly blackberries had closed around her, secreting her away, she'd left her own mark on the eagle, below the raptor's eye. Not that she knew anything about that. She knew only that she was still fast enough. For now. And if the day came that she wasn't, she had a place to go. A place where, for the first time ever, someone missed her. Perhaps that was the meaning of home. A place where you were missed.

As drowsiness overcame her, the image of Mr. Peabody's oak table set with blue plates was already evaporating from Asha's memory, but it hardly mattered. Cats have better ways to recall things. Even surrounded by salty ocean air, Asha could smell the crab cakes and catnip, the tea and cookies, wood fire and wet boots, plank floors with their braided rugs, the quilts, the books, the flannel shirts and woolly winter socks, that empty mouse nest behind the kitchen wall, and the rich aroma of ripe pears lingering in an old pine box. Each scent wrapped itself around her as she sank into the deepest sleep she'd known in days.

The Unpredictability of Friends

A Poem by R. J. Peabody and Rufus

It's funny how
you go looking for one thing…
and come home with a friend.
How wonderful to find
what you wanted most
when you didn't even know
what that something was.
Friends, it seems,
turn up in the most unlikely places,
neither looking nor acting
anything like
we imagined
when we first thought
them up.
The best friends don't always talk a lot,
and yet they fill the silence.
They come bearing gifts
of the sort only time unwraps.
Stories with beginnings you've yet to learn,
and endings you create
together.

Wishes

A Poem by R. J. Peabody and Razi

Making the wish
isn't the hard part.
It's believing.
Believing
even when you don't
really deserve
to have your wish come true.
But wait.
One thing is harder than believing—and that is
recognizing the moment
when your wish is fulfilled.
Somehow it never looks the way
you thought it would.
Or should.
Cherish that moment, for
no imagination, however well fed,
can rival fate
when it comes to surprise endings.

To My Midnight Warrior

A Poem by R. J. Peabody

Secrets can almost never
be kept forever.
You must have known that
when you came.
So your secret
was meant to be shared then.
What a gift.
As humans go,
I may not have been
the best student.
But perhaps you taught me
more than you think.
I know now
that each friend
must be loved differently.
A door, whether open or closed,
lets some friends in—
and others out.
Dear extraordinary cat,
though you'll forever belong
to the untamed world,
we'll keep an extra blue plate at the table
always…
for when you bring your wild heart home.

Mr. Peabody's Special Crab Cakes
A Friend-Tested Recipe

Ingredients

- *1 ½ pounds fresh cooked crabmeat, chunked or shredded*
- *1 cup dried sourdough bread chunks*
- *Half cup freshly grated Italian parmesan cheese (Use a good one!)*
- *2 tablespoons minced green onion*
- *1 tablespoon finely chopped fresh parsley*
- *Salt and pepper to taste*
- *Well-sifted wholegrain flour for coating crab cakes*
- *4 egg yolks*
- *5 tablespoons of the thickest sour cream you can find*
- *1 teaspoon dry mustard or creamy horseradish sauce*
- *1 pinch of rosemary or basil—or a dash of red pepper flakes*
- *1 tablespoon Worcestershire sauce*
- *2 tablespoons fresh lemon juice*
- *Butter and olive oil to sauté the cakes*

Directions

1. *Gently toss together crabmeat, bread chunks, parmesan, parsley, salt and pepper, and other seasonings.*

2. *Beat together egg yolks, sour cream, lemon juice, and Worcestershire. Combine carefully with the crab mixture and form into patties. (If too moist, add more bread. If too dry, add lemon juice or sour cream.)*

3. *Melt a generous amount of butter (or butter/oil mix) in a heavy (preferably iron) skillet over medium heat.*

4. *Dust crab cakes ever so lightly with flour, and place into the skillet as soon as the butter begins to sizzle and snap.*

5. *Brown on each side until the cakes reach what Mr. Peabody calls a golden loveliness—about four to five minutes per side.*

6. *Share with a cat, if you are fortunate enough to know one.*

Vicki Spandel

I hammered out my first book—a mystery about a lost dog—one keystroke at a time on an old Remington my dad kept on the closet floor. I was 6. Have to say, it didn't gain much of a following, but it hooked me on writing forever.

In my professional life I've been blessed to wear many writing hats—classroom teacher, writing instructor for adult professionals, reading and writing coach, telecourse developer, editor, workshop creator, journalist—and a few others. I've had the good fortune to work with thousands of teachers and young writers of all ages, and since my dog mystery days, have written or co-authored forty-some books, most of them on writing or the teaching of writing.

No Ordinary Cat is my first published work of fiction, though it's fiction I love most because in the end, stories reveal the deepest truths about our world and ourselves. This book began with a visit from a mysterious feral cat who showed up one day in our back yard, which borders wilderness. He was gorgeous. Intelligent and wary. Completely mistrusting of humans. Had to be a great story there. He just needed a little help telling it.

As I wrote this book—the most joyful writing I've ever done—it came to me that parts of it had been in my heart and mind for years. Books grow within us, a synthesis of all the bits and pieces of life that have touched us, and might therefore touch someone else. In this book, Rufus appears as a red cat, but behind those mesmerizing green eyes is, I think, the friend we all seek. Maybe he's someone you know.

Jeni Kelleher

I'm Jeni, a pastel artist who loves to create wildlife portraits and custom keepsakes of beloved pets. As I create each portrait, I try to reveal the subject's humor and character. Close-ups allow me to capture the soul in each subject's eyes, something I think is evident in the illustrations for *No Ordinary Cat*.

I also try to ensure that each portrait tells a story. You need to dig deep to make that happen, looking for things not everyone would see. I learned this from my Dad. When I'd take a photo of a flower, he would say, "Now zoom in on it." That's when I'd discover the insect or water droplet I hadn't even realized was there. In nature's secrets, we find both mysteries and answers to all we will ever seek to know.

Remember the goose nest with its six eggs? Like the other pictures in this book, that one tells a story—but you have to look at the little details to discover it. The way the nest is constructed, each piece of straw carefully woven in, shows the ingenious ability of nature to come up with a design that protects vulnerable beings—like little birds nesting on the ground. The down tells us that the parents are close by, guarding their future offspring, providing warmth and protection. We can't see the babies yet, but we can anticipate how those six little goslings will look once they hatch and make their way to the nearby water. The message is one of hope.

This is the second book I've illustrated, and I'm hoping to do many more. To learn more about my work and see additional portraits, please visit me at petportraitsbyjeni.com

Acknowledgements

*N*o *Ordinary Cat* wouldn't even be a book without my visionary friend and colleague Steve Peha, who served as my development editor, publication coordinator, and designer. Before Steve got involved, I'd worked on the manuscript for nearly two years, off and on, but really only thought of it as my writing therapy. I looked forward to settling in at my computer each morning with a cup of coffee, tinkering with my "cat story," as I called it then. When Steve learned I was working on a piece of fiction, he asked to read it, and my whole world changed. He not only urged me to finish it—and publish it—but offered insights and suggestions that were invaluable in turning a sketchy early draft into a story of friendship and courage. Steve, thank you for believing in this project from Day 1, for insisting it was "much more than a story about cats," and for helping me find a whole new voice. What an incredible writing coach you are.

Thanks also to my brilliant illustrator Jeni Kelleher, who has a magical way of letting her subjects' eyes do all the talking. I first saw Jeni's work when I was out and about with friends in Sisters, Oregon, where I live. Her paintings were featured at a local coffee house, and I was so mesmerized by the strikingly beautiful face of one big red cat that I momentarily forgot where I was or why I'd come. "My word, *that's Rufus!*" I remember shouting out to my friends, who had no idea I was even writing a book and therefore couldn't imagine who Rufus was. The universe was with me that day, for Jeni walked in right as I was explaining my emotional response to her art. When I learned it was the artist herself standing before me, the words spilled out before I even thought to say a proper hello: "I love your work. Would you consider illustrating a children's book?" Thankfully, and remarkably when you think about it, she said yes. What a joyful experience this has been, Jeni. Thank you for pouring your heart and soul into making Rufus, Asha, Razi, and their beautiful world come to life.

My sincere appreciation to Dennis Schmidling, manager of Sisters Gallery and Frame, who took extra care in photographing Jeni's artwork for the book. Thank you, Dennis, for treating each piece with such patience and thoughtfulness.

It wouldn't be right not to thank my extraordinary children, Nikki and Michael, as well as my talented guitar playing grandson Jack, for reading aloud with me and listening to stories through the years. You're all to blame for my addiction to chapter books. See what came of it? I love you. And finally, thank you to my lovable husband, Jerry, without whose patience and selflessness I could never have found the time to write this book—or so many others. It's really good of you to tend to the house and garden, make dinner, bring me snacks, and always have a smile on your face. It doesn't hurt that you like the same music I do, either. Believe me, I know how fortunate I am.

CPSIA information can be obtained
at www.ICGtesting.com
Printed in the USA
BVHW021503190820
586573BV00002BA/4